books by
Shigeo Watanabe and Yasuo Ohtomo

I Can Do It All By Myself books

How do I put it on?
An American Library Association
Notable Children's Book
What a good lunch!
Get set! Go!
I'm king of the castle!
I can ride it!
Where's my daddy?
I can build a house!
I can take a walk!

I Love To Do Things With Daddy books

Daddy, play with me!
I can take a bath!

Library of Congress Cataloging-in-Publication Data Watanabe, Shiego, 1928–[Kumata-kun no tanjōbi. English] It's my birthday. Summary: Bear's fourth birthday serves as an occasion for his family to go through the photo album commemorating his birth, his life as a baby, and all his past birthdays. [1. Bears—Fiction. 2 Photographs—Fiction. 3. Birthdays—Fiction. 4. Babies —Fiction.] 1. Ōtomo, Yasuo, ill. II. Title. PZ7.W2615It 1988 [E]—dc19 87-16096 CIP AC
ISBN 0-399-21492-5
First impression

an I LOVE SPECIAL DAYS book

It's My Birthday!

Shigeo Watanabe Pictures by Yasuo Ohtomo

Philomel Books New York

Today is a very special day for Bear.
It's his birthday.

Grandma and Grandpa come to visit and give him
a birthday present. It's his own photo album.

"Who's this?" asks Bear.
"That's your mommy and daddy before you were born,"
says Grandpa.

"Here's Mommy again," says Bear. "What is she doing?"
"She's getting ready for someone very important,"
answers Grandma.

"And here you are, Daddy. Were you going on a trip?"
"That's Mommy and me at the hospital," says Daddy. "We arrived in the afternoon and late that night you were born. The someone important was you."

"I was so small," whispers Bear.

"But you weren't always very quiet," says Mommy.

Mommy points to the album.
"This is your first photo with Grandpa."
Bear smiles. "We're both dressed in blue."

"And here's your first bath with Grandma."
"Now I can take a bath all by myself," says Bear.

"Did I cry a lot when I was a baby?" Bear asks.
Mommy smiles. "Only when you were hungry."

"We are all dressed up here," says Bear.
"That was your first Sunday out," says Daddy.
"We were so proud."

"Here you are when you were one year old."
"What's that on my back?"
"A pillow—to help you walk," says Daddy.

Bear laughs. "It didn't help me, did it?"
"You were still too little," says Daddy.

"Here I am eating spaghetti."
"What a mess!" Grandma laughs.

"Was I a good baby?"
"Most of the time." Mommy smiles. "But look at you in this picture."

"Here you are on your second birthday," says Mommy.
"What did we do that day?" asks Bear.

"We all went to a parade."
"Look, I'm on Daddy's shoulders!"

"Daddy, can I have a ride now? Giddy-up! Giddy-up!"

"Oh, you're getting too big." Daddy laughs.
Everyone else laughs, too.

"Here you are after a bath," says Mommy.
"Rub-a-dub-dub," sings Bear.

"Now what am I doing?"

"You liked to run around after your bath," says Daddy.

"I still like to run around," says Bear.

"But now I'm big enough to put my clothes on all by myself."

"One, two, three candles," counts Bear.
"This was your third birthday."
"What's on my face?" asks Bear.

"You had the chicken pox, so we couldn't go out. But we had a chocolate cake and we read all your favorite books."

"That was fun," says Bear.

Bear turns to the next page in his album, but there is nothing there.

"That's for today's birthday surprise," says Grandma.

Grandma, Grandpa, Mommy and Daddy go to the door.

"What is the surprise?" asks Bear.

"You'll see," says Grandpa with a smile.

Bear can hardly wait.

What a wonderful birthday! Bear, Grandma and Grandpa, Mommy and Daddy, and all of Bear's friends have driven to the river for a birthday picnic.

Everyone sings "Happy Birthday." Bear blows out his candles and makes a birthday wish.

And everyone poses for a birthday picture.
Now Bear will have a new photo for his album.